THE FIELD BEYOND THE OUTFIELD

by Mark Teague

SCHOLASTIC INC.

New York   Toronto   London   Auckland   Sydney

When Ludlow Grebe
began to complain
about the monsters
in his closet,

and the sharks
that swam by outside
every time it rained,

his parents decided
that he needed "something
real to think about."
  So they signed him up
to play baseball.

Ludlow put all of his energy
into learning the game.
   He watched the pitches and
counted the strikes, and hardly
thought about monsters at all.

   And when he finally
got a chance to play outfield
for the Oswald County Hornets,
Ludlow was ready.
   A good ballplayer is always ready.

They told him to play back—
far, far back—to where the weeds
got scraggly and the other players
looked small as ants.

He was so far back
he was almost out of the outfield
and into another field altogether…

…where another
game of baseball
was in progress,
in a towering stadium
topped with pennants
and filled
with monsters
of various types.

It was just what Ludlow
had feared might happen.
   But he reminded himself
that a good ballplayer must always
keep his mind on the game.
   So he watched the pitches and
counted the strikes,
and when the other fielder
asked if he could hit,
he told him that, in fact,
he could.

When the inning changed, Ludlow was whisked off to try his luck swinging the bat.

The monsters in the stands became quiet when Ludlow stepped up to the plate.

His stomach growled, and his legs felt weak....

So he did what all
good ballplayers do:
He tipped his hat
and tapped his shoes,
and grinned
a big-league grin.

The pitcher threw
a fastball with one hand, and
a curveball with another...

...but Ludlow saw
the knuckleball coming,
and he swatted it
out of the park.

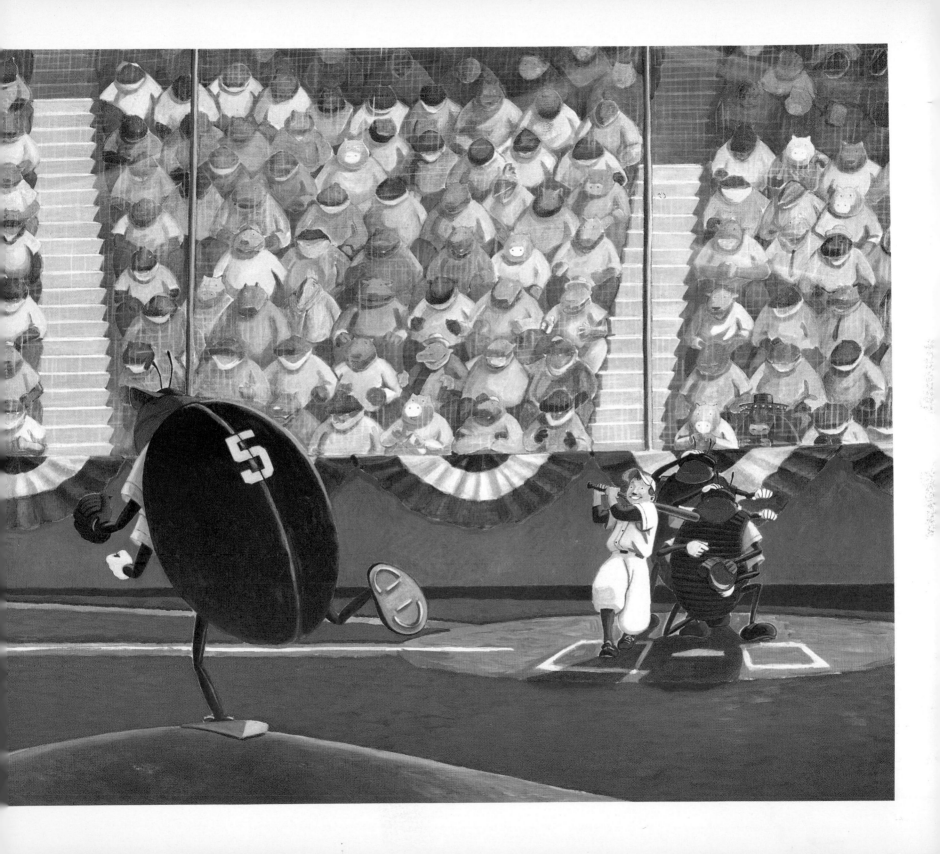

It seemed
like the cheering
would never stop.

But Ludlow had his own game
to get back to, and night was coming on.

His parents smiled at him
when he came in from the field.
"You'll get more action next time,"
said his father.

That night Ludlow went
to bed without complaining,
and the monsters in his closet
didn't bother him at all.
He was ready for what
the next day would bring.
A good ballplayer
is always ready.

For Sarah *and*
Johnny

ISBN 0-590-45174-X

12 11 10 9 8 7 6 5 4 3 2 1   4   4 5 6 7 8 9/9

Printed in the U.S.A.   08

Designed by Claire B. Counihan

The artwork in this book was
painted with acrylic
on paper.